The Magic Patchwork

Written by Mary Lowe and
people from Newcastle upon Tyne.
Illustrations by Emma Holliday.

"Have you been enjoying the summer holidays?" Ella said. "What have you been up to?"

"Nowt."

"Nowt?"

"It's been a bit boring," said Jordie.

"I remember we had a lot of fun when I was your age. We used to get up to all sorts of mischief."

Jordie crunched on his biscuit and sipped his tea. He liked to hear Nanna talk about the old days.

"We used to play in the street. We had a skipping rope that used to stretch across it."

"We'd get mown down by traffic if we tried to do that," said Jordie.

"Let me see if I can think of some of things we used to do... There was hopscotch, rounders… If you saw a car, it was such a novelty you'd take down the number plate. Kissy catchy, monte kitty (like leapfrog only the lads you jumped over were held down by other lads), hot rice, top and whip. To eat, there were sherbet dabs, pipes of Spanish liquorice, bullets, Dolly Mixtures…"

RI, RI.
Chikar I chi kar I
ony, Ony Ompom
    pony.
Ala Pala Basha.
Chinese Chunks.

Jordie looked at his nanna, whose eyes were glistening. He could see the little girl she used to be: a live wire, full of fun, chasing her friends down the street.

"Don't they have the Saturday afternoon pictures any more?" she asked.

Jordie shrugged his shoulders.

"We went to the Raby Picture Hall on a Saturday afternoon but the kids there were so rough. They used to sit on the balcony and pelt you with apple cores while the film was being played. My favourite though, was knocky door neighbour." Jordie imagined his nanna aged ten, dressed in a Scotch kilt and red jumper, tying the knockers of two houses together, before braying on the door and running away.

"And then there was the Spanish City in Whitley Bay. I wrote a lovely story about that once for school." She looked down at the quilt she was working on. "It's here somewhere, a picture of the dome. The Pierrots who used to dress up in costume. Here, look at this." She showed him a miniature painting of a white dome that looked like a temple and people dressed in strange black and white checked costumes.

Then came the question he was dreading.

"Ready for the big school?"

His stomach knotted together. "Nanna, it's the high school."

"Well, are you ready for it?"

"Aye," he said. "Probably." Then added, "Let's have a look at that Spanish City again. When are you going to finish it?"

"Not long now."

"Do you remember I told you about Uncle Arthur with the bump on his head?"

"From when you dropped him?"

"That's the one. I'm starting a childhood scene showing me, Arthur and Betty. I'm ten years old and they're just little and I'm looking after all of them."

On the cloth, drawn very faintly, was the outline of a girl wearing a kilt, holding the handle of a huge pram. Inside were two babies, with their mouths open.

"Where was your mam?" he asked.

"She was way too busy to look after the bairns. In those days if you were the eldest girl you had your hands full helping your mam with the house. I'd have to peel the potatoes, scrub the step, help with the cooking."

"It sounds terrible."

"At least we were never bored. But little Arthur, he was my first baby brother. Born on a Saturday… I heard this screaming and squawking and didn't know what to think. I didn't realise my mother was having a baby upstairs. Then eighteen months later, again on a Saturday, I got Betty. I developed a fear of Saturdays after that."

Jordie rolled his eyes and smiled.

"And to this day," Ella said, "although Arthur is seventy nine years of age, when he's poorly the bump stands out like an egg."

Dickie

Nanna sat stabbing the cloth with her needle and slowly the patches of white were filled with different colour threads and the pictures took shape.

"What's up, lad?" she asked.

"Nothing."

"You're bored, I can tell."

He was silent for a while and fiddled with his hands.

"Mebbes," he said.

"Aye, well," she said.

A minute later she disappeared into the kitchen. Dickie hopped after her, from bookshelf to coffee table to lamp stand. Jordie heard the sound of the tap turning, dishes crashing together in a bowl, and then a gut-snagging, custard-curdling, room-shattering shriek.

"Eeeeee! Jordie, man, come quickly."

Jordie dashed into the kitchen just in time to see a flash of yellow as Dickie flew through the window and away into the street. "You naughty bird! Come back!" shouted Ella through the window. But Dickie merely puffed out his lemon chest and dived into the hedge at the front of the house.

"After him, Jordie!" Jordie rushed out of the house and looked outside through the yellow leaves, the yellow rose bushes, the yellowing grass. Minutes later, Ella struggled out, wearing her hat and coat. "I've phoned your mam and your sister. We'll need as many as possible to get a hold of him."

"But it's all yellow, Nanna," said Jordie.

She handed him a fishing net. "He's done it on purpose," Ella said. "He waited till the leaves turned before making a run for it."

Jordie suddenly remembered that he was out in public carrying a fishing net with his nanna shouting orders at him. He pulled his hood well over his face. If anyone asked, he was a zoologist on the trail of some very rare wildlife.

A flash of yellow headed towards the road.

"There he is!" Jordie shouted, clambering over the wall. The bird had flown towards Scrogg Road Juniors. It flew above the library fence, flitted past the newsagents, scooted over the zebra crossing and flew between the twin brick pillars of the junior school.

"Maybe he fancies a spot of book learning?" said Ella.

Soon the others arrived. Jordie's mam, Stella, and Jordie's sister, Della. They waved their nets in the air like flags and shouted at each other. Della tried to scramble up on Stella's shoulders.

"You go!"

"No, you!"

"Watch me heels."

Jordie was acting cool. He took his duties as wildlife expert very seriously. If they made a commotion the bird would fly away. Anyone would know that. Out of the corner of his eye, he noticed a little ball of yellow. Dickie was standing on a low wall, looking at him. Jordie had an idea. Humming was not one of his talents but he did his best and hummed the *EastEnders* theme song for all he was worth. Miraculously, the bird hopped towards him.

"What's that racket?" shouted Mam.

"Sssssh!"

The little canary hopped onto Jordie's arm and with one swift stroke, was under the fishing net.

Back in her flat, Ella sat stitching her quilt as Dickie sat on his little perch.

"You're a hero, Jordie. That bird keeps me sane. I don't know what I'd do without him."

The
Bird ...
who missed
seeing the sky......

That night he slept in the spare bedroom among the sewing, the balls of wool and painted pictures that would soon be stitched together to make a quilt. His hoodie and shades were placed carefully on a chair. He'd been so busy that afternoon that he hadn't had time to think about school, but there in the darkness the fears came creeping back. He tossed and turned in the narrow bed, thinking about the scratchy new uniform. He thought about the scary new teachers and the miles of corridor he'd have to navigate. Then he drifted away on a river of dreams.

While he slept, a stream of children tumbled through his head. They laughed and chased each other with skipping ropes and prams, throwing apple cores and Dolly Mixtures. A group of lads knelt by a camp fire chewing some half-cooked potatoes. Two children, a brother and sister, looked through the windows of a grocers at a cat which was washing

itself. The children scratched the window and the cat leapt towards them, smashing a display of eggs in the process. They ran off laughing. His dream was a jumbled mass of colour and movement. A little girl with a red jumper and a Scotch kilt stood outside a small terraced house. She cleared her throat and began to read from a piece of paper she held out in front of her.

There were two girls, Sonia and Barbie, who have their fortunes told in Spanish City. They were told by an old Gypsy that they will soon find treasure and get a reward. They looked everywhere. Sonia even looked in her top secret hiding place – behind a loose brick in a wall where she usually hid her sweets.

But they found nothing. A while later, they were digging in Sonia's garden to help her mother when they saw something gleaming. They were amazed to find it was a gold wedding ring. They rushed upstairs to show Sonia's mam and were astonished to see that she was almost in tears.

"That's the wedding ring that I lost two years ago," she cried. She was so delighted that she gave them money to spend on rides at Spanish City; on the Rainbow Pleasure Wheel, the Virginia Reel, the Figure, The House that Jack Built and the Ghost Train.

The little girl in the Scotch kilt grinned, gave another wave and mouthed, "Everything will be alright" before disappearing into the darkness.

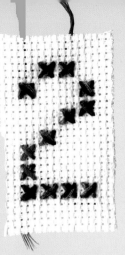

"Give me five, Nan!"

Jordie stood on his nanna's step. He was wearing a parka with the hood pulled up so all you could see of him was a little red nose and feet sticking out at the other end.

"Five what?" said Ella, who'd come to the door dressed in her coat.

"How about five pounds?"

"Daylight robbery," his nanna snorted. "I'm ready to go, are you?"

Jordie was giving his nanna a bit of a treat. He was staying with her for the weekend as Mam and Della were away on a shopping trip. His mam had given him extra pocket money and he wanted to celebrate with tea and cakes at a posh café in town.

They took a bus to City Road and admired the bridges that stitched the banks of the Tyne together; the Tyne Bridge, the High Level, the Swing Bridge and the Blinking Eye Millennium Bridge. They took in lungfuls of sharp cold air that was laced with salt.

"Look at this place now," said Ella, as they walked past an office block.

"There used to be a soap factory here. This is where I used to pack Drene shampoo, dressed in a white overall and hat. I loved that job."

"I thought you worked in a dressmakers, sewing tags on belts."

"I've done all sorts. In those days, you could get a job as easy as anything. I also worked in Parsons, the engineering works. I was making cut-outs that were stuck to pieces of machinery. When we got bored we'd take it in turns to take a faint so we'd have to go out for fresh air."

Jordie had an idea. Since he'd captured Dickie, he'd had no more luck as a wildlife expert and was beginning to fancy his chances as a historian instead.

"Nanna, could you help me with my history project? We have to write about people's jobs in the old days and what they did in the war."

They were walking through the entrance of the Posh Stottie tea shop and Nanna's nose twitched.

"Ahhhhh," she said, "all in good time. Sniff that fresh coffee and look, they have chocolate eclairs!"

Over the next half hour, Ella chomped her way through two chocolate eclairs and a flapjack. Jordie demolished a piece of chocolate cake and a cream doughnut.

"I don't feel well, Nanna," he groaned.

"I'm not surprised. All that sugar at your age. It's not good for your teeth," she said, revealing a set of perfectly white false teeth.

"Let's be ganning."

At home, Jordie slumped in front of the TV, nursing his stomach.

"Do you want any toast, pet?"

"Nanna, you must have a cast iron belly!"

"That's me, brought up on dried egg that tasted like rubber."

"Nanna, about that history project…"

"Howay, man, Richard and Judy are on in a minute."

Jordie slumped further down into his chair. Gangster, wildlife expert, historian, Jordie didn't seem to be able to make a go of any of them. A while later his nanna was poking him in the back.

"C'mon, you're making the place untidy. Get yourself away and have a proper sleep." She held up the patchwork quilt. "Nearly finished. Have a nap and all your worries will disappear."

She wrapped him in the quilt and led him out of the sitting room.

Jordie lay wrapped up warm, dreaming. He heard voices and saw boys wearing flat caps and girls in long skirts. The voices unravelled like silken threads and twisted through the air above him. Some were strong and booming while others were gentle and quiet. Clouds of golden dust swirled behind his sleeping eyes and turned into undulating khaki sand dunes. A soldier wearing a red beret waved at him. "You want to know about how we lived in wartime? How about this one then?" he said with a smile.

One day as me and my mates were driving through the desert on the way to the petrol depot, our truck broke down. We tried to mend it, tried all sorts but couldn't. Then a figure came into view, he looked like a twelve-year-old boy, wearing a black turban, with dark hair and eyelashes. He appeared like magic and told us his name was Iousha. He took us back to his village where his uncles fixed our engine but while we were having something to eat we heard gunfire. "It's the brigands," said Iousha, "Help us please!" Luckily we had our rifles, and after firing a few warning shots the brigands ran off. Later we waved goodbye to Iousha and drove off into the sunset.

The soldier leapt into a truck and started the engine. The sky darkened and he heard the sound of a siren and in the distance, the rat-a-tat-tat of gunfire.

The room grew chilly as Jordie scanned the sky, looking for planes. Suddenly they were flying up the Tyne, silvery and agile like angry birds, followed by the sound of shrapnel bouncing off the roofs.

"Quick!" a voice said, "Hide under here."

Someone handed a tiny baby to her mam and dad as they stood at the entrance of an underground shelter.

"Ugggh," spluttered Jordie. "Get off me."

He pushed back the quilt, feeling as if he were suffocating. He smelled the damp earth and saw the white cloud of breath from the family in the shelter. He thought he was about to be buried underground.

Ella popped her head round the door. "Are you alright?"

"Nanna," he whispered. "I've just had a nightmare. It was awful. I dreamt there was a war and a soldier from the British army told me a story about a desert ambush."

Ella shrugged, "Oh, that'll be Molly's husband. He was stationed in Egypt."

"And then there was a family who were about to go underground in a shelter, there were bombs dropping out of the sky."

"That might be Nancy. It's one of her earliest memories."

"But why did I dream about it?"

Ella looked at him and her brown eyes softened. "It's the magic of memories, lad. You'd be surprised. All the sights and stories me and my friends could tell you about, they've been painted onto the quilt."

Jordie sat up straight in bed. "Well, c'mon then, Nanna. You tell me and I'll write them down for school."

But Ella just winked at him and said, "You keep coming round for visits and you'll soon have more than enough for your project."

Jordie muttered under his breath and looked for something to keep him occupied. He watched TV, played with his Game Boy and cleaned out Dickie's cage. Ella was unusually quiet. "Are you feeling alright, Nanna?" asked Jordie.

"Aye, just a bit of heartburn. I'll be champion before long. Too many cream cakes," she said, patting her stomach.

At bedtime, Jordie studied the quilt some more. There were dozens of pictures – miniature paintings and embroidered patches featuring people wearing old-fashioned clothes and the sort of toys he'd only ever seen in a museum.

"I wonder…" he thought. And he settled himself down, pulled the quilt over his head and fell asleep. In his dreams he saw a young girl wearing a white overall, blowing bubbles into the sky like diamonds. A black and white dog wandered up a road, followed by a van.

A voice with a chuckle bubbling underneath it, told the story.

xxxxx was a butcher's messenger, taking all the workmen's dinners to them, but sometimes the smell of the meat brought the dogs running. I had a Bedford van which fell to bits, then a Mini van with Cooperative Butchers on the side. I used to have to go up fourteen flights of stairs to deliver half a pound of mince. I was often in a hurry, for the shipyard wives wanted their meat before 12 o'clock as they had to make a pie crust for the dinner. One time I looked out of the van and I saw the meat running up the street! I chased it but the dog got away. I said, "The dogs's got a mouthful." My boss said, "Whose meat is it?" and I said, "I don't know – the dog can't read the paper!"

Jordie groaned and turned over. Suddenly the dream switched to the inside of a shop, where a little girl, about four years of age, stood behind a counter on a box that had the words 'Puck Matches' written on the side. She took money from the customers as she handed over newspapers and comics.

It was a wholesale newsagents, the first one in Gateshead. We sold confectionery and toys and so on. I soon became quite a help in the office as well, counting the money and putting it in the bags supplied by the bank. Counting the gold sovereigns was quite an

experience! When I was about eight, after leaving school for the day, I used to take the small carriage over the High Level Bridge, which was a half penny each way, to meet my mother in town. Our business was on the main High Street and there was a jeweller facing us. They had a huge clock in the window and within a short period of time I was able to read it.

The clock beside Jordie's bed read six o'clock. The sun was resting just beneath the horizon as the night turned to dawn. The birds began their wake-up call. As Jordie began the journey back from dreamland, the figures on the patchwork quilt became still.

When he woke up, he yelled for his nanna and pulled the quilt tighter around him. "I need a pen and paper," he said.

A few weeks later, Ella was sat stitching her patchwork quilt when the phone rang. It was Jordie.

"Nanna, I got my project back. I got ten out of ten, the teacher said I'd done a lot of research and it was really good."

"See, I told you."

"But I didn't do any research, Nanna. I just fell asleep."

"You're a good listener, Jordie. That counts for a lot. You can pick things up, that's what's important."

"I just wanted to thank you, Nanna, you and all the other ladies who made the pictures. Next time I see you, I'll treat you to tea and cakes again."

"Don't worry about that, pet," she said and turned back to her sewing.

She only had a few patches left before it was finished. It was the best quilt she'd ever made, shot through with the vivid colours of her life, the characters she'd known as a child, memories of friends and family. There were so many people she missed. There was her own mother and father, her daughter Jacqueline, who was no longer with her, the lads and lasses she'd known when she was growing up.

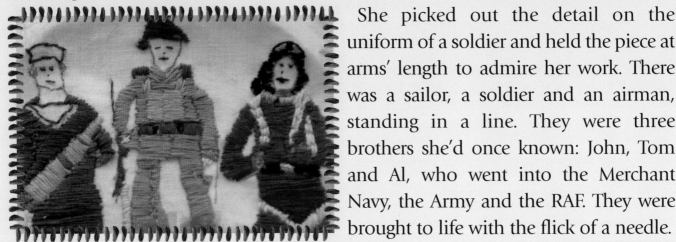

She picked out the detail on the uniform of a soldier and held the piece at arms' length to admire her work. There was a sailor, a soldier and an airman, standing in a line. They were three brothers she'd once known: John, Tom and Al, who went into the Merchant Navy, the Army and the RAF. They were brought to life with the flick of a needle.

Her fingers ran over the surface of the quilt until she found a picture of a man with ruffled hair. She smiled to herself at Uncle Billy Best. Ella closed her eyes and her lips began to move.

Uncle Billy Best worked in the Team Colliery in the winding engine room. He knew every bit of the engine, the levers, the pulleys. The winding engine had a big wheel driving a belt, which made sure that the pit was full of fresh air that the miners could breathe underground. There was a smell of machinery, oil, heat. It was humid in there and there was a constant chugging and clicking. Billy and his mates would say, "Get thee pipe!" which meant go have a rest. You always saw him with an oily rag.

Winding Engine House

The special thing about Billy was that he looked just like Stan Laurel, a famous comedian, who was part of a double act called Laurel and Hardy. He even used to get dressed up as Stan Laurel and go on the stage. He made us laugh all the time. Stan Laurel and Oliver Hardy were so different. The fat one was pompous and the little one was like a scrag-end. The climax came when the *Evening Chronicle* had a competition for Hollywood doubles and he sent in a picture of himself dressed as Laurel. I came in from school one day and Mam was excited as her brother had won the competition and had to go to the Empire Theatre to be presented with a prize.

It was warm in the room and Ella wanted to lie down. She'd been feeling so tired recently. She'd had a lovely life, but she knew that her time was nearly come. She settled in the chair and pulled the quilt around her. She saw a horse and cart filled with people singing their hearts out. She saw a garden swing where she used to play and a music teacher barking the words, "Ella, come bring your music!" She was at school again, a tiny girl in a pinafore dress, standing in the corner of a large classroom, her left hand smarting from the teacher's ruler. A big tear rolled down her cheek. She wanted someone to cheer her up, to tell her everything would be alright.

"This'll have you smiling," said a voice, "Remember that time I dug up those old bones and took them to the Police Station, saying I'd found some murdered bodies?" It was her favourite brother, Joseph, who was standing beside her. His cheeks were rosy and his pockets bulged with conkers. "And remember the time the show folk brought a whale to the Town Moor? The smell was awful!" Joseph held his nose. Ella rubbed her hand and started to laugh. The corners of the room melted away and she saw a mass of faces swirl by; her neighbours, friends at the Church Hall, Jordie, Della and Stella. And suddenly she and Joseph were sitting drinking tea from china cups.

"I remember the day you scaled the Seven Bridges down at Willington Quay, that huge viaduct that crosses a stream running into the River Tyne. Coming home from school that night, I saw a crowd of children cheering a young boy who was 'making the climb' to prove how tough he was. I thought, 'Stupid boy, you wouldn't get one of my brothers doing that.' And as I walked over, my heart nearly stopped. It was you! It took you over an hour but you did it. One false step and that would have been the end. After you got down, I ran to you and hugged you but you said all you could remember was the slapping I gave you."

Joseph laughed. "We were young and daft in those days, weren't we?"

"So why are you here then, Joe? I've not seen you for ages."

"I thought you needed a bit of company, pet."

"You're not going to take me away, are you?" asked Ella, timidly.

He smiled. "Not yet, Ella. You have a little while to go."

She shivered and stared into her teacup.

"It was awful when you went away. You said, 'Love you, Ella, the show is ended.'"

"I know."

"All that life snuffed out."

They sat and drank their tea in silence.

"Except… it's not, is it?" said Joseph. "We leave parts of ourselves behind. Memories. Being with others and loving them. That's enough to make our mark on the world."

Ella looked up and smiled, "You're right, Joe. You always did speak a lot of sense. Here…" She reached over and touched a piece of the quilt as it lay wrapped around her knees.

"It's the viaduct and there's you, a tiny figure." She rubbed the piece of quilt.

"It's here forever," she said. "It's indelible."

"And every time you tell young Jordie about the past, you're bringing it to life," said Joseph.

Her brother's face was flushed with the warmth from the fire. Ella could still smell the tang of the river from that day seventy years ago. She heard the cheers from the children mixed with the cry of the gulls that wheeled overhead. Her brothers and sisters, mother and father, her daughter, were all gone, but she knew how she could keep them alive. She pulled the quilt up around her shoulders and began to softly snore.

The End